For Patch —F.B.
For Kyle Zimmer and First Book —L.N.

If You Give a Dog a Donut

Balzer + Bray is an imprint of HarperCollins Publishers.
If You Give a Dog a Donut
Text copyright © 2011 by Laura Numeroff
Illustrations copyright © 2011 by Felicia Bond

Library of Congress Cataloging-in-Publication Data is available.
ISBN 978-0-06-026683-7 (trade bdg.) — ISBN 978-0-06-026684-4 (lib. bdg.)

11 12 13 14 15 LPR 10 9 8 7 6 5 4 3 2 1 ❖ First Edition

is a registered trademark of
HarperCollins Publishers

If You Give

a Dog a Donut

WRITTEN BY **Laura Numeroff**

ILLUSTRATED BY Felicia Bond

Balzer + Bray
An Imprint of HarperCollins Publishers

If you give a dog a donut,

he'll ask for some apple juice to go with it.

When you give him the juice, he'll drink it all up.

Then he'll ask for more.

There won't be any left, so he'll want to make his own.

He'll go outside to pick apples.

When he's up in the tree, he'll toss you one.
Throwing the apple will make him think of baseball.

He'll want to play.

You'll have to get a ball

and a glove.

Of course, he'll also need a bat.

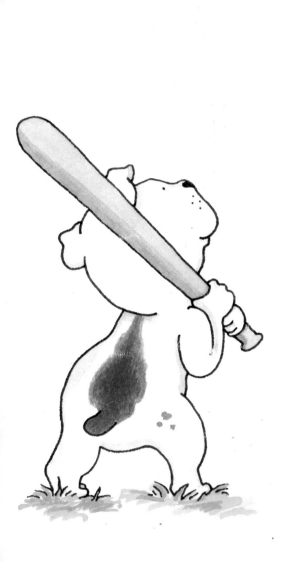

He'll ask you to pitch.

He'll hit a home run!

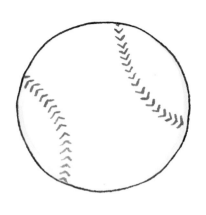

Then he'll do a happy dance to celebrate.

Dancing will make him hot and dusty,
so he'll need some water.

He'll probably start a water fight.

You'll have to dry him off with your bandanna.

He'll wrap it around his head and pretend that he's a pirate.

Then he'll want to go
on a treasure hunt.

He'll find an old kite and want to make one himself.

You'll have to get him some sticks, paper, and string.

When the kite is finished,

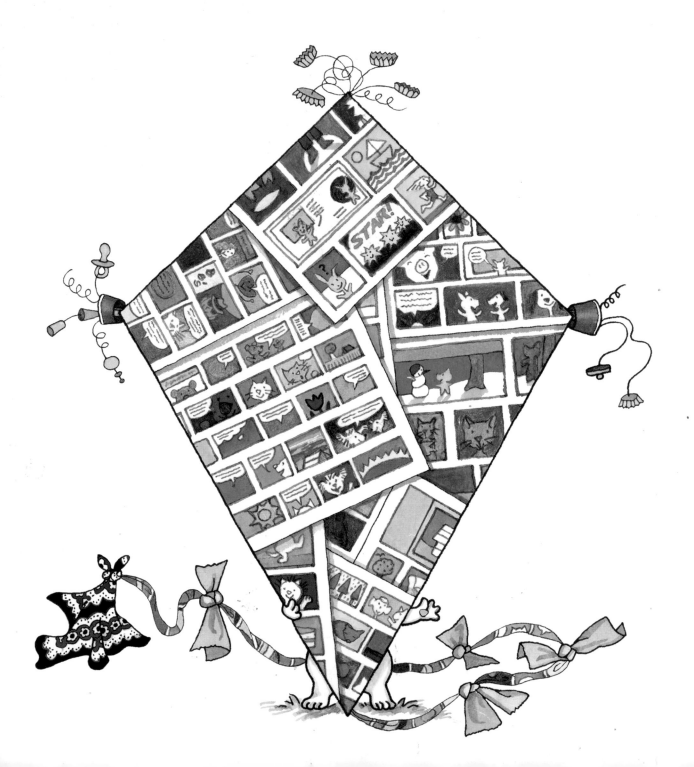

he'll want to fly it.
It will go higher and higher,

until it gets tangled in the apple tree.

The tree will remind
him of apple juice,
so he'll probably
ask you for some.

And chances are,

if he asks for some apple juice,

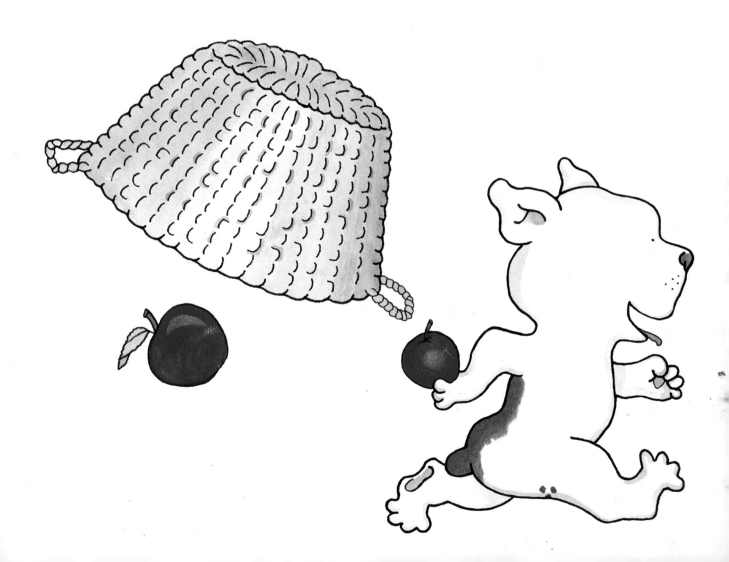

he'll want a donut to go with it.